This Starfish Bay book belongs to

....

AN UNLIKELY NEST

Written by Yimei WANG
Illustrated by Dandan ZHU
Translated by Courtney Chow

Jumpy was a very hasty kangaroo. One day, she jumped too quickly and hit her head against a small tree.

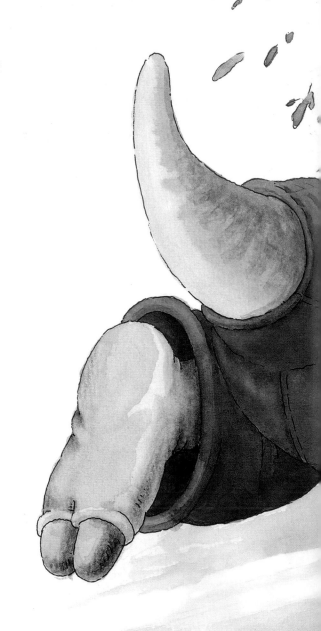

If she had hit a normal tree, then there would be no story to tell. But Jumpy wasn't a lucky kangaroo. She had hit a small tree that housed a nest of birds.

"I never would have thought that birds would live in such a small tree," Jumpy said.

"As long as it's a tree, birds can live in it." That's what Father Bird had said to Mother Bird when he first chose this tree.

Mother Bird was usually tweeting, but at that moment, she was very quiet. Such a dangerous accident was bound to have happened sooner or later. But Father Bird found living in such a low tree very convenient for flying to and fro, so he was unwilling to move.

"Whoever ruined my home will have to pay for it!" Father Bird held on to Jumpy.

"Pay? I'll have to pay for your nest?" Jumpy became worried. "Oh, why is it I'm so unlucky? Alright then, I'll go find some straw and mud. Just wait here." Jumpy positioned her tail in the right direction and prepared to jump off.

"Wait a minute." Father Bird held on to Jumpy tightly. "My family needs a safe place to shelter from the storm."

"Okay," Jumpy replied. "Then how about you go and shelter in the cave first? I hide my food there, and it's never gotten wet at all."

"That won't do," Mother Bird piped up. "We're not food. We can't stay in the cave. It's too cold there."

"Okay," said Jumpy. "How about staying in the tree hollow? I've hidden my shellfish coins there. It's very safe."

"That won't do either." Mother Bird was even unhappier. "We're not money. How could we stay in such a boring hole?"

"Then... what can I do?" Jumpy had no idea these
birds would be so hard to please.
Father Bird suddenly circled Jumpy, staring at her
pouch in amazement.

"We'll just stay in your pouch." Father Bird's suggestion
was exactly what Mother Bird was thinking.
Even if Jumpy didn't want it, her pouch had already
become a bird's nest.
"I can only hope this will only be temporary..." Jumpy
mumbled as she jumped off to find straw.

The family of birds no longer wanted to move. It was so warm and safe in the pouch! Most importantly, this was a bird's nest that could jump and move. There were so many unexpected benefits of this nest. Just take yesterday. Jumpy had hopped to the cinema, bought one ticket, and watched a movie. Meanwhile, the birds were also brought into the cinema and watched a movie for free.

But when Jumpy entered the buffet, the manager said,
"Please buy five tickets."
"Why?" Jumpy didn't understand.
"It's because you've brought along four birds,"
the manger replied.
"But they're just staying in my pouch. They
aren't here to eat," Jumpy explained.
"I don't care. Everyone who enters must buy a
ticket," the manager insisted.

So that she wouldn't go hungry, Jumpy bought five tickets. "If it's this
expensive every time I eat, I'll soon go broke!" she said.
The bird family was well-fed. There was no need to even describe how
happy they were.

The two baby birds slowly grew bigger. They began to learn how to sing. As Jumpy was taking a stroll through the forest, the two baby birds started to sing. Listening to their song while strolling was such a lovely moment. Jumpy was mesmerized by their delightful tweeting.

In the evening, Mother Bird sang a lullaby. She sang it over and over again, but the two baby birds wouldn't fall asleep. Meanwhile, Jumpy felt dozy and yawned ten times in a row.

Bang! She hit another tree.

"Luckily, this tree doesn't have a bird's nest." Jumpy felt a little confused after the collision. Before her mind cleared, a swarm of bees rushed toward her.

Oh no, she had hit a tree with a beehive! It would be no good if the bees wanted Jumpy to pay for their beehive and moved into her pouch, too.

Jumpy escaped hurriedly, but the bees chased closely behind.

From her pouch, the bird family yelled, "You can do it, Jumpy!"

Jumpy could hop no longer, so with a loud
splash, she jumped into a stinky lake of mud.
She rolled around in the muck. Jumpy had
turned into a smelly, stinky kangaroo.

The bees couldn't stand the stench, so they flew away, buzzing.
The bird family couldn't stand it either, so they decided to move out.
"We'll find a big, sturdy tree to live in," Mother Bird said.

"We'll still stay in your pouch sometimes, but we'll make sure Mother Bird doesn't sing any lullabies," the baby birds reassured Jumpy.

In the following days, Jumpy was able to go to the cinema alone, eat at the buffet alone, and go for strolls alone, just like she had always enjoyed. She felt free and happy! There was also another new thing that she liked doing...

And that was visiting the bird family at their new nest!
She sped up, thinking, "This time I won't knock over their home!"

Starfish Bay® Children's Books
An imprint of Starfish Bay Publishing
www.starfishbaypublishing.com

AN UNLIKELY NEST

ISBN 978-1-76036-068-9
First Published 2019
Printed in China by Toppan Leefung Printing Limited
20th Floor, 169 Electric Road, North Point, Hong Kong

Text Copyright © 2012 by Yimei WANG
Illustrations Copyright © 2012 by Dandan ZHU
Originally published as "袋鼠的袋袋里住了一窝鸟" in Chinese
English translation rights from Tomorrow Publishing House

Sincere thanks to Elyse Williams for her creative efforts in preparing this edition for publication.